Published in 2014 by Simply Read Books
www.simplyreadbooks.com

Text & Illustrations © 2014 Clare Pernice

Library and Archives Canada Cataloguing in Publication

Pernice, Clare, author
    Circus girl / Clare Pernice.

ISBN 978-1-927018-36-1 (bound)

    I. Title.

PZ7.P44Cir 2014   j813'.6   C2013-905184-8

We gratefully acknowledge for their financial support of our publishing program
the Canada Council for the Arts, the BC Arts Council, and the Government of Canada
through the Canada Book Fund (CBF).

Manufactured in Malaysia

Book design by hundreds & thousands

10 9 8 7 6 5 4 3 2 1

CIRCUS GIRL

Simply Read Books

for Mia

circus girl

a story of make-believe

words and pictures by
clare pernice

a leotard

socks

and a girl

to the sound of
APPLAUSE

the
CURTAIN
goes up

T A

D A !

it's

circus

girl

the poetic spectacle
begins with a

j^ump

she's **daring** and

dazzling

and Oh! so

dramatic

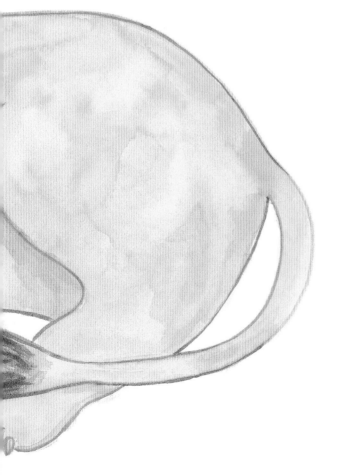

and completely

OUTRAGEOUS

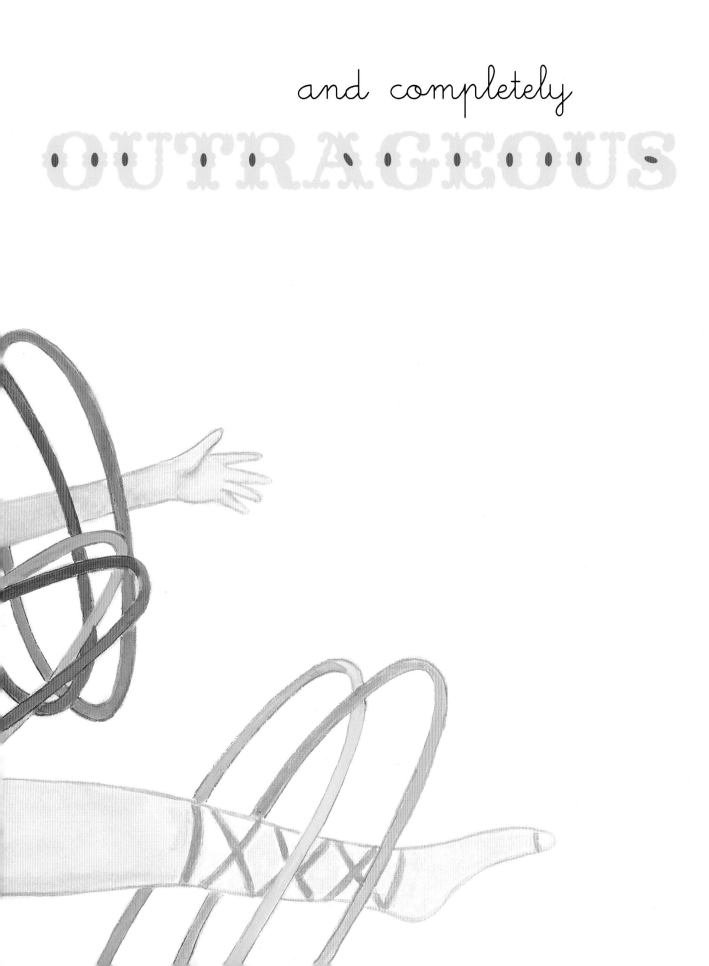

she's

PLUCKY

BOLD

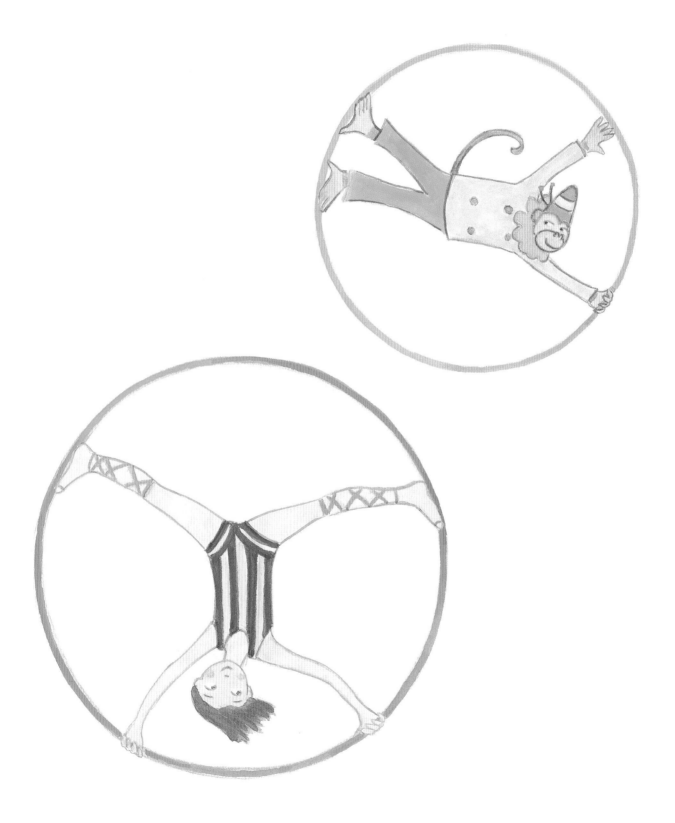

and

Oh!

so

AMAZING

she truly has

talent

she's

★cîrcus
g★îrl

star

of the show